MY NAME IS AMERICA

THE JOURNAL OF RUFUS ROWE

A WITNESS TO THE BATTLE OF FREDERICKSBURG

BY SID HITE

Scholastic Inc. New York

BOWLING GREEN,
VIRGINIA
1862

⭐ ⭐ ⭐

SEPTEMBER 22, 1862

My name is Rufus Rowe and I am sixteen years old. Most people looking at me do not believe my age, as I am skinny and smaller than average. I had rickets when I was a boy. My chest sinks inward and I walk bowlegged. Saying so is not asking for pity. It is stating a fact. It's also a fact that I'm much quicker and stronger than I appear.

It seems a shame to put words in this fine, leather-bound book Miss Brooks gave me two months ago. The paper is of such a quality I have never seen before. But here I have already started, and it is not too much a shame, for Miss Brooks said when she presented me the book, "This is a parting gift, Rufus. You spell and punctuate better than anyone I ever taught, and you show a keen promise with your letters. These are historic times we live in. If you keep a record of what you see and hear and we are so fortunate as to meet again in the future, I would be interested in reading what you wrote."

Miss Brooks said that on July fifteen, eighteen sixty-two. It was a Tuesday. I know because it was two days after my birthday, which fell on a Sunday. Funny thing was, Miss Brooks did not know my birthday was near. She gave me this book because she is a generous soul. She also gave me a pair of wool socks to keep my toes warm in the coming winter.

When Miss Brooks said "historic times," she was speaking of the War between the Northern states and the Southern states. The North calls itself the Union, and we in the South call ourselves the Confederacy. Mostly people just say Yanks when they mean the Union Army and Rebels when they mean the Confederates. The War has been going on now for one and a half years. So far the South has been teaching the North a mighty lesson. By that I mean the Rebels are winning.

I guess Miss Brooks is not Miss Brooks anymore. By this late date she must be Mrs. Something-or-another. I hope she is happy being married and living in Richmond. I did hate to see her go. She was the best teacher I could ever hope to know.

Today is a Monday. I'm starting my journal because I decided to leave Bowling Green and do not trust to tell anyone but this book. Bowling Green holds only grief for me. My no-good father took off when I was two and left Momma to fend for herself and me. She did alright, considering the lack of paying work around here. We were poor, but happy enough, until about the time I turned ten and Mister Jeffrey Jenkins came asking for Momma's hand in marriage. I argued against the man, but it was Momma's decision to make, and after some months she wed Mister Jenkins. That was the beginning of rotten times for me. Sometimes I think the man married Momma just so he would have me to kick around. He is meaner than a cornered snake, but not so foolish as to ever lay a rough hand on Momma. I reckon he knows what I would do if he ever hit her. All that said, I am done with his hollering ways and am planning to run off as soon as I judge the time right.

I intend to wink Momma on the matter before I

slip off. I won't tell her any details of where and when I'm going, and she won't ask, but she'll understand. We've talked before about me making my way in the world.

It feels good to have made up my mind. Nothing can be worse than the six years I have spent doing everything wrong in Mister Jenkins' eyes.

SEPTEMBER 30

The replacement teacher for Miss Brooks arrived in Bowling Green yesterday and we started back to school this morning. The new teacher's name is Miss Howlett. She pins her hair flat to her head and never smiles. I was willing to let her win my favor, but all she did today was show her ignorance of manners. She talked harsh to Gertrude over nothing. Gertrude is only eleven and cries easily. Miss Howlett's arrival determines me to leave here soon.

I grant Miss Howlett one thing, she is knowledgeable about the goings on outside Virginia. She told us about the proclamation Abraham Lincoln claimed he would sign in the coming year. It is supposed to make slaves as free down South as they are up North. Miss Howlett said the Northerners have divided opinions on the matter. On one side is a group called the abolitionists. That was a new word on me. It stands for the people who argue against slavery and have been pressing Mister Lincoln to destroy the South. On the other side of the argument are the pacifists. They want Mister Lincoln to make terms with the South and let us go our own way.

They can argue all they want up North, but the truth is, the people down South don't appreciate being told what they may or may not do. Mister Lincoln can sign his proclamation any day he wants, but it won't mean much unless the Yanks win the War, and they have a long way to go before doing that. So far they've lost every big battle except the fight at Antietam Creek, which the Richmond newspapers called a draw.

October 5

It's Sunday and Mister Jenkins just switched me for nothing more than burning a batch of biscuits. In a way, I'm glad he did that because his action has determined my date for leaving. I'm going with the sunrise tomorrow.

I hope the old coot has a proper fit when he wakes up and finds me gone.

It's night now. My way of telling Momma what I'd planned was to ask if I could inspect the haversack she keeps in her closet. When she gave it to me she said there was something inside I might find use for. I looked and found ten dollars in silver coins, so I know Momma knows I aim to leave. The money is in my pocket now, and the haversack is in a tree alongside the Fredericksburg-to-Richmond turnpike. I plan to be up and gone before the milk is delivered.

Aside from Momma and Gertrude, the only other person remaining in Bowling Green who I might miss is Thornton Scott, who is a thirty-year-old man who keeps the records at the courthouse. He'd be off fighting with the Rebels if he didn't have a gimp left arm. When Thornton settles on a subject, he likes to sit on it until he's done. Being as I like talking, too, we make a good team, and have spent many long hours together discussing the hostilities that divide us from the North. Thornton always says "hos-tilities" instead of saying "war."

October 6

It's afternoon and I've been walking north toward Fredericksburg since dawn. A stagecoach raced past a while ago. Other than that, I have seen no one else on the road.

I picked Fredericksburg as a destination because it is a big town and I believe Mister Jenkins will search for me in Richmond. He knows how much I respect Miss Brooks and will figure I followed after her.

I just ate a boiled egg and an apple. I have another egg and two more apples in my haversack. I'm also carrying five biscuits, a cut of cheese, a blanket, my winter hat, a wool coat, two shirts, a pair of pants, the socks Miss Brooks gave me, my vocabulary book, a quill, four nibs, and an inkwell. My money is in different pockets and in my shoes.

I aim to walk a couple more miles, then find a place to bed down for the night. That way I can enter Fredericksburg in the morning. Having never been there, I think it best to first see the place in broad daylight.

OCTOBER 7

It's late morning and I've not gone far from where I slept because I stopped to put down about the Rebel scouts I encountered on the road near Smith-field. That's a big slave farm that I had heard people talk about but never saw, until today. The scouts were friendly and did not seem too disappointed when they asked if I had any tobacco and I said no.

One of the scouts was riding the most beautiful black mare I've ever laid eyes on. He said the Yanks that were in Fredericksburg last summer were long gone now and the town was plenty safe for travelers like me.

Seeing them scouts made me regret my size. I know a boy from Bowling Green and heard of another from Milford who joined the Army of Virginia when they were fifteen. I envy the adventure they must be having serving under General Robert E. Lee. That man is smarter than three Union generals put together. Most people say when the South wins the War the credit will rest with Robert E. Lee, although some argue for Stonewall Jackson. He is a general, too. But that's off my subject. Just a minute ago the scouts galloped west toward Massaponox, so I reckon it's time for me to head into Fredericksburg.

OCTOBER 10

I entered Fredericksburg three days ago and I'm writing this at a table outside the Rising Sun Tavern. That is a stagecoach stop where a person can buy hot food. I paid ten cents for a bowl of beef stew and two hot biscuits. That is high spending for a meal, but I was feeling empty and do not regret the money gone.

There are more people in Fredericksburg than I ever imagined. A man I asked told me the town had a population of four thousand people. Although I've had no luck finding a position yet, I expect I will soon. Also, the crowd suits my purposes for not being tracked down by Mister Jenkins.

I slept the last two nights against a wall behind the Apothecary Shop on Caroline Street. Each day I walk around asking store proprietors if they need any help. So far they have all said no, but I won't allow that to set me back. Like the old saying goes, "Rome wasn't built in a day." That means to keep trying until you get what you're after. At least that's what it means to me.

OCTOBER 14

Fredericksburg is full of prosperous people who keep informed of events. I ate inside the Rising Sun Tavern today and listened to some men talking about Jeb Stuart and the cavalry riding circles around the Union Army. Jeb Stuart is a general who established his name riding raids in the Shenandoah Valley. A fat man with a top hat was telling how Jeb skirted the whole Yank Army last week, crossed over the Potomac River, and destroyed property as far north as Pennsylvania. Then two days ago, Jeb Stuart brought his troops back to Virginia without losing a soul. After saying that, the fat man predicted the whole War would be over in six months. Everybody agreed they hoped he was right, but none in the room seemed so confident as the fat man.

I've been walking around asking for a position so many times that people are beginning to say, "Hello Rufus," when I pass by. That is better than being a stranger. I feel I have made a start.

I found a house on Princess Anne Street letting beds for ten cents a night. It is an extravagance, I know, but I will go there tonight so I can wash up in the morning. I have to hawk-eye my money from now on. I have only been in Fredericksburg one week and am already down to nine dollars forty cents.

It is fine fall weather we are having.

OCTOBER 17

I may have had a lucky turn. I was buying an apple this morning and met a girl named Peg who was all smiles toward me. When she bought a bushel bag of apples, I asked why so many apples, and she said she worked in a mansion with plenty of mouths to feed. I explained how I was looking for a position, and Peg offered to inquire into the matter. She gave me directions to a place called Brompton and said come by tomorrow and she would tell me what she learned.

Brompton is on Marye's Heights, up above Telegraph Road. I have to follow Hanover Street out to Telegraph Road, then cross Sunken Road where there is a stone wall, and then climb a hill. I am supposed to go there in the early afternoon. Peg said to look for one of the slave men out back and tell him I came to speak with her.

Peg spoke with a funny accent. The man selling apples told me she was an Irish lass. I guess Peg is thirteen or fourteen years old.

OCTOBER 18

I climbed the hill up to Brompton about ten o'clock this morning and did not see anyone stirring out front. I stopped to survey the place. It is a two story, brick house with wings on both sides and four white columns holding up a roof in the front.

I went around back and found a tall negro who laughed when I told him I was seeking Peg. I asked him why he laughed and he said, "No good reason," then went to fetch Peg.

Peg came out and told me there was no need for help, but Eveline said I could fix a bed above the stable. I asked Peg who Eveline was and she said, "Mister John Marye's youngest daughter. I am hired as her companion and sometimes I help Lottie the cook. Eveline said if you stay here, keep yourself scarce because her father would say no if she asked."

Peg left and I saw a girl peek from an upper window. I figured it was Eveline. The tall negro came and led me to where the horses are kept. There is a room up top with nothing in it but a three-legged table and a barrel to sit on. I have tired of sleeping on the sly in town and decided the room was a fit.

I fixed a bed with straw and my blanket. At dusk the tall negro brought me a biscuit, two candles, a box of strike matches, and a ragged quilt no one would bother missing. We got to talking and I learned his name is George. He is old enough to have some white hair. He said there were fourteen slaves on the farm, but only him and two slave women in the house. I asked what the farm raised and George said corn, potatoes, and pigs mostly. He said Mister Marye was a lawyer and his wife was dead. Eveline has two older brothers in the Confederate Artillery and five sisters who got married and moved away.

OCTOBER 19

It was strange waking up this morning to the sound of neighing horses. There are four of them all told. I heard someone come downstairs and take them out just after dawn, but did not make my presence known in case it was Mister Marye.

I went outside and peeked around a couple of times and went to the outhouse, but I mostly spent the whole day being scarce as I was advised to do. About dark I was starting to think staying here might not be such a good idea. Then George came with two ham biscuits that he said Peg asked him to deliver and I changed my mind.

I hope Momma is not fretting over my where-abouts. One day I will write her a letter and say I am doing well.

OCTOBER 20

I'm sitting in my room with two candles burning. George brought me some flat bread and showed me where the chickens were cooped in case I want an egg. He is a good man. I've not seen Peg or Eveline for two days.

This morning I went to town looking for work and met a soldier from Mississippi named Charlie Kent. He gave me two cents for running to buy him a pouch of tobacco. The army gives it out, but Charlie said it never smokes smooth as store-bought. Charlie is with the regiment guarding the riverbank. There are sixteen hundred men in his regiment. They have been digging rifle pits along the banks of the Rappahannock and watching for Yanks. Charlie said he has seen plenty of cows and stray dogs, but no Yanks. He reckons the Union Army is sitting around Washington twiddling its thumbs.

I spent another ten cents at the Rising Sun Tavern. I can recommend the beef stew. The place was here before the Revolutionary War for Independence. I know about that war because Lafayette marched through Bowling Green on his way to Yorktown. He was a French man who helped the Colonies fight the British.

There is a nip in the air tonight and I'm wearing my coat as I write this. I miss Momma a bit, but am mighty glad to be free of Mister Jenkins.

NOVEMBER 2

It is hard to believe I have been thirteen days without writing a word. I have been sleeping here at Brompton and going every morning to visit Charlie Kent. People from Mississippi are real jolly and polite, too. Charlie introduced me to everybody in his unit and now I have a regular business taking orders and fetching articles from the stores in town. The fellows give me a little extra over the price when I deliver. They ask mostly for coffee, tobacco, and sugar. I've earned ninety-eight cents in coin since I started my service. All the soldiers call me Mister Rufus.

Today is Sunday. This morning Eveline came with Peg to my room before church. It was the first time I spoke face-to-face with Eveline. She is pretty and has fine manners, although she is quite prissy by the standards to which I am accustomed. She said she would pray in church that I find a position in town. When I told her I already had an enterprise going, she smiled as if she did not believe it so. I made no effort to persuade her of anything. Eveline said her father knows I am here, but is pretending he does not. I suspect it is true because I saw Mister Marye two days ago in the yard and he looked hard my way. I nodded as if we were acquainted, and he turned away without responding.

Peg left two green apples on my table before she and Eveline departed for church.

Then this afternoon George brought me a bucket of hot water to bathe with. Before I did so, I asked if he was named after George Washington. George said he didn't know, but he might be because George Washington grew up at Ferryfarm, which is just across the river from Fredericksburg. Later on he married a woman from here named Martha. George Washington, I mean. Not the George I know. He doesn't have a wife.

After I bathed and changed my shirt, I took the bucket to the kitchen door and gave it to George. He said I looked better clean than dirty. I told him that was good, as I now had a business in town fetching supplies for the soldiers. George said he was impressed with my gumption.

NOVEMBER 3

I went to town this morning and saw Charlie Kent. We sat for a while on what remains of the old railroad bridge and were not saying much of anything, so I asked Charlie why he thought there was a war. He said there were several reasons. One was state's rights, which is a fancy way of saying people from one place cannot order folks from somewhere else what to do. Another cause was the say-so of the cotton growers who don't want to lose their slave labor. Then Charlie told me the Yanks call slavery the Peculiar Institution, and I said I'd never heard the term before. He said the Yanks were full of terms no one ever heard before, but he wasn't in the fight over terms. He put on a uniform because the Yanks had marched south with guns and it was a man's duty to defend his homeland. I asked, "So for you it's a matter of honor?" and Charlie said, "It is indeed." We were quiet again, then Charlie asked why I thought there was a war. I told him, "I'm only sixteen, so this is just an opinion, but it seems to me the North has an idea about what is proper and the South has another idea, and the two sides are fighting because their ideas are different." Charlie gave me a long, up-and-down respectful look when I said that and reckoned that I put my finger on the plain truth. I try not to let things go to my head, but Charlie's saying that made me feel mighty good about myself.

NOVEMBER 7

It turned cold last night, then snowed all day. I'm thankful for my coat and hat and the wool socks Miss Brooks gave me. They keep me way warmer than the Mississippi boys guarding the riverbanks. What they have for boots is pitiful and their coats aren't much better. The men keep fires going day and night, but I still see them shivering when I pass by on business. I felt so bad today I bought a bag of licorice from the Apothecary Shop with my own funds and passed it around a fire where Charlie was standing. Lieutenant Kershner was present and remarked on how I was a credit to the South. Everybody cheered, "Hear hear." I turned red at that.

Seeing as I earned twelve cents today, I stopped in town before heading back to Brompton and bought a gray scarf to keep my neck warm. It cost me fifteen cents. I looked at some wool socks that cost twenty cents, but they weren't as thick as the ones Miss Brooks gave me, so I kept my money.

NOVEMBER 9

There is a slave who comes every morning for the horses. After he took them out today he came back to clean the stalls and I went down to look on. He said, "Morning, Rufus." I inquired how he knew my name and he replied, "'Cause you're George's friend. My name is John." I grinned a bit and asked was John Brown his hero. He said, "Yep. How'd you know?" and I answered, "Just guessed." John worked a bit and I watched how he pays a lot of attention to what he does, then out of the blue he told me Mister Marye was not so bad as some masters.

This evening when I got back from town my room hardly smelled of horses. John did a fine job.

George came with beans at nightfall and I told him what John said about John Brown. George nodded and looked sad. I asked why and he said, "They hung John Brown."

After George said good night and went, I sat wondering what he meant when he said, "They hung John Brown." Did he mean "they" as in "everybody"? Or was he saying "they" to speak of the Confederacy?

I suspect George meant the Confederates hung John Brown. It is true, plus I can't imagine he would have much sympathy for our side.

★ ★ ★

November 13

It is warm today and hard to believe there was snow on the ground last week. Charlie Kent told me the Union Army has a new general named Burnside that Abe Lincoln appointed because the last general was afraid to fight. I remarked that maybe the old Yank general was smart enough to know what would happen in a fight with Robert E. Lee. Then Charlie said something that surprised me. He said, "Let's hope this one is smart that way, too."

I guess Charlie is brave enough to be a soldier and do what's asked of him, but not very eager to be shot at. It makes sense to me.

A while ago I was thinking I'd not seen Peg or Eveline for a spell when they came to my room and presented me with a sweet potato. We sat talking and Eveline complained the War was making it difficult to get the things she wanted. I didn't ask what things, as I didn't care to know. She doesn't appear to be suffering anywhere I could see. I suspect Eveline has been spoiled. She's kind enough, though. She told Peg to take a box of candles from the pantry and put them in my room tomorrow. I said, "There's no need for that, Eveline." Then she said, "The candles are a gift, Rufus."

After Peg and Eveline left, I ate the sweet potato in three seconds flat. When it was gone, I wished I had another.

November 17

Big news! Thousands and thousands of Yanks started arriving across the river in Falmouth today. Everybody thought they were camped somewhere near Warrenton, but they must have moved because they are here now. I guess that Burnside fellow is more ambitious than the man he replaced. The whole town is worked up wondering what will come next. There is no one to stop the Yanks from crossing the Rappahannock but Charlie's regiment and some artillery troops scattered about on high ground. It would be thirty Yanks against one Rebel if they attacked now, or worse, since the Yanks are still coming on foot and with wagon loads of supplies.

When I went down to take a look at the Yanks, Charlie advised me to get away immediately and said so in a tone that did not brook argument.

On my way back to Brompton I saw a crowd at the Presbyterian Church on Princess Anne Street. I imagine they were praying for the Yanks to turn around, as no one believes they came here for a picnic.

I heard shooting late in the day, but not much. Before it got dark George came to fetch me and we walked over to Telegraph Hill. That is south of here, beyond the Willis house. Telegraph Hill affords a long view across the river, and there were other people up there watching when George and I arrived. We saw tents going up for as far as the eyes could see. It was a strange feeling, looking at all those Yanks and knowing they came with guns for shooting Rebels and anybody else that got in their way. It made me think there are some things I don't understand about people.

On the walk home I asked George what he made of the situation and he said, "It don't bode well for peace and quiet."

The horses are snorting and stepping about in

their stalls below me. They seem to know everybody is nervous tonight. I am going to put out the candle, but I doubt I will soon fall asleep.

I wonder if Miss Brooks knows I fled Bowling Green. It appears as if I am soon to witness some historic times up close.

November 18

Peg came this morning before I had time to wake up. She said Mister Marye was not taking any chances and they were going to stay with kinfolk at Forrest Hill. I asked where that was and she said somewhere toward Caroline County, probably on a hill. I thought that was a ridiculous answer, but did not share my opinion, as it was not a time for small talk. Anyhow, Peg ran out before I could have spoken. Her help was needed packing things in the house.

Right after Peg left, John came to the stable with a slave I never saw before and pulled the buckwagon into the yard. I put my boots on and went outside, but returned to my room when I saw Mister Marye and three slaves carrying trunks to put on the wagon. A minute later John came back for the horses and led them out to the wagon.

I spent most of the morning sitting on my barrel, watching the comings and goings through a crack in the wall. Seeing Peg and Eveline and Mister Marye preparing to leave made me feel so rotten I did not bother to move when they boarded the wagon and departed. Now I regret not running out and waving good-bye to Peg and Eveline. They have been kind to me.

It is damp and cold tonight. I'm going to warm my toes over a candle before I put on my socks and get in bed. I am worried for Charlie Kent and the other Rebels picketing the riverbank. They are close enough to smell the Yanks.

NOVEMBER 19

George stayed to watch the house for Mister Marye, and it is just me and George living here now. We laughed at the oddness of that. George recommended I take a bed indoors. I told him I would accept another blanket if there was one to spare, but I was cozy in the stable. George said take two blankets if I wanted. I took one.

We heard musket fire around noon, then it started to rain. I did not go into town. This evening George and I had a fine meal of ham and beans on the front porch. The rain ceased after dark.

November 20

The Yanks are still collecting in high number, but have not moved across the river. I guess they are organizing before they try to take Fredericksburg. Poor Charlie Kent. Brave as those Mississippi boys are, sixteen hundred of them can't stop a whole army.

George and I were sitting on the porch a while ago when a Rebel officer came on horseback and informed us he was taking over Brompton. George said he was in charge of watching the house and the man said fine, just don't get in the way. I did not approve of his tone so I inquired who he was. He said Corporal Welsh. He has a reddish goat beard, but doesn't look much older than twenty. He claimed he was here to establish headquarters for Major General Lafayette MacLaws. I asked what good was a headquarters without an army to fight the Yanks. That was when Corporal Welsh gave the glad news that Robert E. Lee and the whole Confederate Army were on their way. I remarked it was about time as the people of Fredericksburg were nervous. The corporal allowed they had reason to be. My first impression not counting, he seems a decent fellow. He hails from Staunton, Virginia.

George shook his head after the corporal departed, and he said, "You know what his coming means, don't you, Rufus?" I looked unsure of my answer, and he said, "From now on things will be changing out of control at Brompton."

November 21

The Rebel Army started arriving this afternoon and are coming in even as I write this down. I have to say, it makes me happy seeing all the gray uniforms.

We have General Longstreet's corps setting up around Brompton. That is who MacLaws reports to, because a general is above a major general. I'd never heard of General Longstreet before, but I spoke with a boy from Georgia who is about my age and he said Longstreet was a hero. I asked was Longstreet greater than Robert E. Lee, and the boy said no one was greater than Lee. The Georgia troops are setting up by the stone wall at the foot of the hill here. I wish I had asked the boy his name.

I went this evening to find the Georgia boy who spoke to me. I did not see him, but I met a captain named Brainard Nelson. He told me the Georgia troops were under General Cobb, and afterward he asked if I knew the Yanks had sent a message yester-day for Fredericksburg to surrender. I said that was news to me. Captain Nelson snorted and said it was not likely the Confederates had marched all this way to give up. I allowed that was my thinking and asked if General Lee was in Fredericksburg. Captain Nelson looked blank and inquired if I was a Yank spy. The question made me pretty hot and Captain Nelson laughed as if he were being tickled to death. Afterward he told me General Lee would likely be here tomorrow.

When I left Captain Nelson and started up the hill,

I heard a soldier say how considerate it was that some-one built a stone wall right where they wanted one.

A picket stopped me in the yard and said I could not pass. I lied and claimed to be living at Brompton for two years. When he still did not let me pass I told him I was friends with Corporal Welsh. The picket claimed not to believe me. Then, like some kind of miracle, I saw Corporal Welsh in the yard and hol-lered. He waved and hollered back, "Hello, Rufus." The picket begged my pardon and told me to go on my way.

George came to my room at dusk and said the presence of so many Rebels was making him itchy. I asked if anyone had done him harm and he said no, the officers in the house were gentlemen. He was itchy, that was all. A feeling came over me that George is my friend and I would not tolerate anyone mistreating him.

I hope Charlie Kent and the rest of the Mississippi troops are alright.

Whew. That was a lot of writing. My hand has a cramp.

November 22

It is a great day and a sad day for Fredericksburg. It is great because General Lee arrived here sometime last night and sad because this morning General Lee advised the citizens to pack their belongings and leave town. No one is surprised by the terrible turn of events. One look across the river at all the blue uniforms tells everyone why they must go. No one but the generals knows if the fighting will start tomorrow or commence the day after, but it is certain a battle is coming. There is nothing but the Rappahannock between the two armies, and it is neither a wide nor a deep river. In most places a man could throw a rock to the opposite bank without much trouble, and in some places a regular-sized person can walk from bank to bank without getting their shoulders wet.

I don't know why the Yanks sat over there for five days without moving. I'm glad that is the case, though, as it has allowed time for the Rebel Army to get here and protect Fredericksburg.

I'm excited to think I might get a look at Robert E. Lee. If I do, then I can say I've seen the Savior of the South. People say General Lee does not smoke, does not drink, does not gamble, does not own slaves, and does not complain. The man is known for loving his home state of Virginia. He rides a big white horse named Traveller that is probably the most famous horse in the world. I've seen more than a few drawings of General Lee and Traveller in the Richmond newspapers.

It's late afternoon now and I just returned from Plank Road, where I was watching the people stream out of Fredericksburg. It was a woeful sight. Some of the richer folks rode in buggies or on wagons, but everyone else was on foot and weighed down with all the valuables they could carry. To make things worse, the road was rutty and slippery after the recent rains, and many of the older people could hardly move forward for stumbling and stopping to get their balance. It was a trial just watching them pass by. I saw one little girl carrying a doll that was half her size. The girl was maybe five years old and struggling hard to keep apace of her big sister and ma. It struck me almost to tears, watching that little girl. You could see in her face how determined she was to get her doll to safety. It left me thinking war is an awful thing, no matter what the reason.

Mister Marye was smart leaving Brompton before the crowd clogged up the road.

I'll probably sleep bad tonight, but I don't care. Witnessing things you don't want to remember is the price of being curious.

NOVEMBER 23

Yesterday evening when I got back from Plank Road I asked George what he was going to do now that a fight looked certain. He said he was going to stay put as long as the house stood. When I told him I'd do the same he grew serious and said, "Don't you have a momma in Bowling Green?" I answered, "That's true," and he said, "You ought to consider going there until the trouble clears, Rufus."

I thought a while and told George I appreciated his concern, but Bowling Green was no place for me these days. He rubbed his chin and bobbed his head. Then I said, "I can't rightly leave you to watch

Brompton by yourself." "Why can't ya?" he asked, and I told him, "There's no use arguing with me, because I'm not in a mood to listen. I'm staying and that's it." Maybe it was a foolish decision on my behalf, but it was worth making it to see the smile that broke across George's face.

I probably shouldn't say this, but George's smiling made me feel so good I stepped over and hugged him real quickly. I've never touched a colored person before, and I wouldn't have done so if anyone was watching, but it came natural and that's what I did. The truth is, George is a good person and there are plenty of white folks I'd trade for him in a minute. There. I said it. George is my friend equal to anybody.

Another reason I decided to stay at Brompton was I don't want to miss the action. Plus, if I went back to Bowling Green now, it would be the same as telling Mister Jenkins he was correct in his ways with me. I'm as inclined to admit that as the Yanks are likely to invite the Confederate Army across the river for a square dance.

November 24

When I got up and going this morning George told me Mister Marye's son had come calling just after dawn. His name is Edward and he is stationed over on Prospect Hill. I suppose he received permission to pay his family a visit, although none were here. I wonder what Edward thought when he saw Brompton, for it is a madhouse with officers coming and going, and mules straying in the yard, and soldiers standing around smoking and waiting for someone to give them orders. The confusion suits me. I find it interesting.

Today I watched the Washington Artillery set up nine big guns in the yard. They look like cannons, only they are bigger with longer barrels and reportedly shoot much farther. Corporal Welsh told me the two biggest guns were called Parrot Rifles. He also explained that the sandbag walls the artillery men built around their guns are called redoubts. The redoubts don't appear to me they would provide much safety against a cannonball, but then I am a newcomer to battle, having never been fired upon myself. I trust the gunners know what they are doing. Anyway, while we were standing there observing the artillery unit, Corporal Welsh told me to look on the porch if I wanted to see Major General MacLaws. When I did I saw a stocky fellow with a bushy beard and wild hair. The major general had his arms crossed and the look on his face was mighty grim. That means nothing, though, as lots of folks around here are wearing serious faces.

NOVEMBER 25

Last night I woke up because the chickens were squawking. When they did not cease making noise, I put on my shoes and went out to see what was bothering them. Turns out it was Rebel soldiers — I saw two of them walking over the hill with a sack when I approached the coop. Then I counted five hens in the coop, which makes four missing. Before I could decide whether to chase after the thieves or not, they were gone, so I felt around in the straw and found five eggs. They are for George and me, unless I can get to town and give one to Charlie Kent. At first I thought what a sorry thing it was for a

Confederate soldier to steal hens from Southerners. Later though, it struck me that this was what happens when there is a war. At least I know Rebel stomachs are being filled. Some of those men appear as if they've been lacking regular meals.

Another day passed with no Yank attack. It is very cold tonight and there are many fires with Rebel soldiers huddled close around. It's a true shame the Confederacy can't provide warmer clothes for its fighting men.

Earlier today I cleared up a matter that had been a source of confusion for me. It was about all the generals people keep naming and the question of are they equal. I asked Corporal Welsh about the matter and he said there are brigadier generals, lieutenant generals, and major generals. The important ones are the division commanders. They are Stonewall Jackson and James Longstreet, plus Jeb Stuart, who commands the cavalry. The main general who stands over the other generals is just a general, and that of course is Robert E. Lee. I don't know if the Yanks name their generals the same.

NOVEMBER 26

I woke up almost frozen this morning. After I got myself thawed out and going, I tried to take a fresh egg to Charlie Kent in town. Down below the hill I had to walk a wide sweep around a regiment of Rebels digging trenches. They were in the woods between Brompton and the little canal that runs there. I got around them and was drawing near town when I ran into another regiment of Rebels that told me to get gone or be shot. They were rough-looking devils, and when I asked why I had to go anywhere, one of them said it was their policy to shoot scallywags. I took offense at that and asked the man how did I know he wasn't a scallywag. He raised his musket and pointed it at me for an answer. There was nothing for me to do then but turn around. I'm not so dumb as to argue with a devil carrying a gun.

On my way back to Brompton I stopped at the stone wall and visited Captain Nelson. He was drinking coffee and offered me some. Not wishing to tell him I despise coffee, I took a cup to be polite. Pretty soon I recalled the egg in my coat pocket and gave it to Captain Nelson. You might have thought I gave him gold, he was so thankful. He broke the egg straightaway and drank it raw from the shell. After a bit I asked Captain Nelson what in the devil the Yanks were waiting for and he said there was a rumor they had forgot to bring their pontoon bridges for crossing the river. He remarked that they could have waded the fords above town the day they arrived, but it was too late now, as Jeb Stuart's cavalry was positioned in the woods, just waiting for them to try.

While Captain Nelson and I were talking I saw the Georgia boy I had spoken with before. The ingrate passed by as though I was not sitting there in plain view. He probably thinks he is better than me because I am not in uniform. That's how dumb some people are. He has himself an attitude without even knowing who I am.

I should mention the North Carolina regiment that is strung out behind the stone wall next to the Georgia troops. They meet more or less straight down the hill from the stable where I'm living. There must be a law in North Carolina that all men have to wear a beard, because everyone I've seen so far has one. Even the boys my age have some kind of scraggly fuzz on their faces. Nothing against North Carolina, but I never saw such an ugly group of men in my whole life. I have to say though, they do appear capable of fierce fighting when and if the time comes, and everyone reckons that will be soon.

When I got back to the house George was worried about where I'd been all day. I said I'd been across the river preaching to the Yanks and got up quite a collection. George wanted to be mad at me, but he could not and we had a laugh together.

NOVEMBER 28

I heard some men talking on the porch as to how Abraham Lincoln had visited General Burnside across the river yesterday. I would like to have seen the Union president. They say he is a gangly fellow and the Richmond papers always draw him looking like an ape. I suspect the president probably told Burnside to get on with the fight or he would throw him out like he threw out the other general that was afraid to tussle with Robert E. Lee.

Corporal Welsh came up while I was listening to

the men on the porch, and after they broke up he offered with some pride that he had carried a message to Telegraph Hill this morning and had seen General Lee. I asked did he see Traveller, too, and he said, "Sure enough, Rufus. I saw them both." Then Corporal Welsh asked if I had ever seen Chatham. I said no, what was that? He explained it was a plantation house across the river that the Yanks were using for headquarters. You can see the place clearly from Telegraph Hill with a spyglass. The twist on this is that General Lee had gone courting at Chatham when he was a young man. He was successful, too, as he married the girl who lived there. Her name is Mary Custis Lee. Corporal Welsh and I agreed it must stir up strong feelings in General Lee to eye the house now and know it is full of Yanks.

November 30

Someone came and stole the last of our chickens in the night. Either that or they disappeared into thin air, which is not likely. George is not too pleased. He is fond of eggs.

DECEMBER 2

General Stonewall Jackson arrived yesterday with more than thirty-five thousand soldiers and started taking up positions south of here. That shows how much I know. I thought Stonewall Jackson was already here. I heard someone say Stonewall had been nearby all along, but was dawdling on the road so the Yanks would think he and his troops weren't available for the fight. Anyhow, he is here and his coming has added a great number to the Rebel cause.

The engineers have been cutting lanes through the woods behind the house here, and now Major General MacLaws has his troops practicing movements. I am sitting in the sun watching soldiers pick up from one position and run to another. I guess MacLaws wants to be ready if the Yanks try to flank around the hill.

It is a mystery why the Yanks have not attacked. Each day that passes only helps the Rebels. Maybe the Yanks are waiting for more troops, but I do not think there are more to have, as Corporal Welsh said a hundred and forty thousand Union soldiers are sitting across the river. The Rebels have eighty-five thousand present. When you think about it, that is plenty of mouths to feed. I don't know about the Yanks, but there are wagon loads of flour, pork, potatoes, and beans coming and going from here every day. There is a whole unit of men just for dividing and cooking the food and getting it to the fighting men. I don't suppose our hens made much difference.

December 4

I awoke last night in a sweat, having dreamed about the little girl carrying her doll on Plank Road. She was crying in my dream and I wanted to offer her some comforting words, but I couldn't open my mouth. It was a long time before I got back to sleep, and only then after I prayed for God to watch over the girl and her doll.

I am down to one candle tonight and must remember to ask George for more. Corporal Welsh said there was a skirmish on the riverbank south of town today. It did not amount to much.

DECEMBER 8

Sometimes I hear shooting in the distance, but it is only musket fire and nothing much has happened so far. I am getting tired of always expecting the fight to start. It wears you out wondering.

I sure wish I could get my hands on a sweet potato like the one Eveline and Peg brought me that time. Thanks to George, I've been eating all the gruel I want. Gruel fills the stomach, but it is not what anyone could call satisfying.

I got a bucket of hot water from the kitchen this afternoon. First I cleaned myself, then I washed my dirty socks and a shirt. After that I walked down to the stone wall and watched the Georgia men playing cards. Captain Nelson did not participate in the game. When I asked why not, he said cards were against his religion. Then a sergeant I'd never seen before declared that Captain Nelson did not play cards because he was regular at losing when he played. I made no remark on the matter, but Captain Nelson kind of grinned as if what the sergeant said might be true.

December 9

Corporal Welsh told me about something odd that happened yesterday evening. He said a Union band stood on the far side of the Rappahannock yesterday and played "The Star Spangled Banner" for all the Rebels to hear. Our side listened in silence while the Yanks played that song and two or three more. Then the band struck up "Dixie" and played it pretty well. That brought a wild burst of cheering from the Confederate side of the river. I asked Corporal Welsh was that true and he said, "Yes, it happened." I suppose it makes sense, as the Yanks and Rebels often holler back and forth at one another across the river. Still, it seems strange to me that a Yank band would play such a Southern song.

December 11

This morning the mist was so thick you could not see twenty feet in front of your nose. When the sky cleared there was plenty of shooting from the direction of town. George and I sat in the yard and listened for hours. One officer looked at us and shook his head like he thought we were something foolish. George and I agreed we do not care what the soldiers think.

George brought me supper this evening and said he heard the Yanks started laying a bridge over the Rappahannock and the shooting we heard was Rebels trying to stop them. George said, "You know what the bridge means, Rufus. They coming." Then he made me swear to keep low when the fighting starts. I swore I would and he said, "You lucky anyway. You most likely be fine."

I sure hope I'll be fine. I don't imagine anyone will shoot me on purpose when the fighting begins. Still, with thousands of men aiming rifles in different directions, I'm sure accidents will happen. Keeping low is good advice. It's exactly what I plan to do.

December 12

It is drizzly and foggy again this morning, but no one is thinking about the weather because the Yanks completed their bridge last night and fought their way into Fredericksburg. Finally, they have made a move.

I have no way of knowing what happened to Charlie Kent and my other friends in the Mississippi regiment. I've not seen them for nearly two weeks. Knowing them as I do, though, I'm sure they held off the Yanks for as long as possible.

It's about ten in the morning and the sky just cleared as if someone pulled a string. I fetched my journal and am sitting outside the stable on a barrel. There's so much musket fire in the distance, it sounds like hail on a tin roof. Now and then the Yanks fire off their big guns, but the Washington Artillery is quiet. That's because Robert E. Lee is not the sort of man to shell a Southern town, even if it is packed thick with Yanks. I can see the Rebel gunners now. They are standing by their redoubts, smoking and looking in the distance.

A fellow who does blacksmithing for the troops just walked by and asked was I writing a book. I said, "You bet," so quick it left him wondering if it was true.

My stomach is turning cartwheels with excitement, but I'm not afraid for my safety, as I know there are a mass of Rebels between town and Brompton. There's that mean bunch of Rebels I encountered the other day, the ones in the trenches near the canal, and the troops below the hill here on Sunken Road. I don't worry too much for their safety, either, as they have that stone wall to crouch behind.

It's night now and the rain has started again. George told me this afternoon to sleep in the house. I said I would, but came to my room instead.

Just now I did something strange. I wrote my name and my mother's name and "from Bowling Green, Virginia" on two different slips of paper. One I folded and put in one of my boots. The other I folded and put in a coat pocket. I hope there is no cause for anyone reading what is on the paper, but if so, it was not much trouble and may make things easier for someone. The reason I put one of the papers in a boot is because coats are the kind of things that get stolen in winter.

★ ★ ★

LATER

I got up now in the middle of the night because I just remembered something I want to put down. I saw Corporal Welsh this evening and asked how the Mississippi regiment had fared against the Yanks. He said they'd delayed the Union advance with heroic bravery and withdrew before they were overrun. That was what I had hoped to hear. The corporal also reported there were so many Yank troops it took them all day to cross into town on their pontoon bridges.

Corporal Welsh never would admit it, but I could see he was nervous about tomorrow. I pretended not to notice anything off about his mood and asked what he was thinking. He said he was thinking about his girl back home. I asked her name and he said Liza Chapman, then he said he was mostly thinking about the Old Dominion, which is another way of saying Virginia. I said, "Oh?" and he said, "Yeah. It's a good place to call home." When I asked how he meant that, the corporal started naming presidents. First there was George Washington, who spent a lot of his boyhood just across the river up at Ferryfarm.

Then came Thomas Jefferson. Then James Monroe, who had a law office right in Fredericksburg. Also, James Madison and Zachary Taylor were born within a day's ride of Brompton. That's a lot of presidents to name without even claiming Jefferson Davis. He's the president of the Confederacy and lives in Richmond. Plus, everyone knows Robert E. Lee hails from Virginia.

I suspect talking about the Old Dominion was Corporal Welsh's way of bucking himself up for tomorrow. The Yanks coming to our side of the river pretty much spells there will be action.

I doubt I'm the only one wide awake in the middle of this rainy night.

December 13

It's cold as it can get this morning. I heard horses stirring and men calling back and forth before dawn. When I went out to see what all the fuss was about, the fog was thick enough to cut with a knife. On my way to the house I heard some soldiers saying the Yanks had torn up Fredericksburg last night. How the soldiers knew that at such an early hour, I don't know. I reckon it's true though, as such things go hand in hand with war. I returned to my room to write this in my journal and now I'm going out again. As soon as the fog lifts I ought to be able to see something from the crest of the hill here.

Later

I'd been sitting in the yard for more than an hour when George found me and gave me an apple. While we were talking about how cold it was, two things happened. First the fog lifted and then three artillery guns on the hill here boomed and puffed smoke. I wish somebody had warned me, as I nearly jumped out of my skin when the guns thundered. George put his hands over his ears and went back to the house. I stayed to write this.

Not a minute ago the Rebel Artillery was answered by the Yank guns and I heard something stream past my head. Now so many big guns are thundering, my ears are ringing, and I can't separate the echoes from the actual booms. Except for the artillery here at Brompton. I can separate that sound, as I see the smoke and smell it, too. This must be how a battle commences.

LATER

Everything above was written this morning. Now it's night and bitter cold. I have so much to put down I don't know where to start. First I'll say there are more dead Yanks beyond the stone wall than I could count. It was a terrible day of events. I don't think I'm exaggerating to say there are more dead soldiers in Fredericksburg tonight than there were living people before everyone left. My mind is in such confusion I hardly notice I am almost frozen solid. I do not know what happened in other places, but we witnessed a great slaughter around Brompton. The fighting stopped hours ago, but I still hear musket fire in my head. I expect to smell gunpowder for the rest of my life.

I'll never say everything I saw today in one sitting, so I will start with what happened after I wrote in my journal this morning. At about half past eleven I went down the hill and spoke with Captain Nelson. He and everyone else were lined up against the wall, at the ready. We could hear artillery and muskets crackling in the distance, but at that point it was calm up and down the wall. Some of the Georgia troops were smoking pipes and writing letters, and I saw one man reading a Bible. Brigadier General Cobb rode past and glared in my direction, and Captain Nelson said he was going to have to ask me to leave. I was planning to do so when we saw a whole division of Yanks march into the wide field on the far side of the wall. They disappeared for a second or two below a rise in the ground, then appeared again and kept coming toward us.

The Washington Artillery up on the hill started in on the charging Yanks when they were well out in the open. I should have retreated then, but my feet would not move and I could not stop looking at the advancing soldiers. They came to within a hundred yards or so of the wall before the Rebels opened fire and felled a whole line of them at once. I wish I had not seen that. As it was, I did not see much more, because Captain Nelson soon whirled around and threw me on the ground. Muskets were firing, men were giving the Rebel yell, artillery was thundering all around me, and when I couldn't take it any longer, I jumped up to run. I glanced over my shoulder as I took off and saw what must've been two hundred Yanks laid out dead in the field. The poor men never stood a chance. I was running without watching ahead and nearly tumbled over a dead horse. That scared me so, I flew up the hill.

I hate to say it, but I saw some dead Rebels at the stone wall. Not many compared to the Yanks, but more than a dozen.

What I witnessed was only the first of many Yank attacks. All day long I could hear them charging that wall again and again. At least I know Captain Nelson was alive at noontime.

My hands are numb with cold and so much else happened between noon and now, I am going to stop writing and put down what else happened tomorrow. That's Lord willing, of course.

DECEMBER 14

I read what I wrote last night and see I did not tell the horror of things. I reckon that is my failure with words. Remembering yesterday makes me wonder how people can be so murderous. No idea in the world is worth such a slaughter. Whoever gave the Yanks orders to charge across that field at a stone wall lined with sharpshooting Rebels was not in possession of a clear mind.

Yesterday after I flew up the hill I saw George coming out of the stable where he'd been looking for me. He said come into the house and took the liberty of grabbing my arm. He didn't have to tug as, after seeing what I'd seen, I was eager for the protection of the brick walls. George and I went up to a bedroom on the second floor. It was my first time going upstairs and I stood in the window trying to look down the hill. If I were taller, I may have been able to see the wall, but as it was I could just see the far side of the field where fresh Yank troops continued to gather. All nine of the guns in the yard were booming and now and then killing some of those troops. George had just told me to step away from the window when eight Rebels burst in the room and knocked the glass out of both windows. They lined up two at a time and fired, then stepped back and reloaded while the others fired.

It didn't take long before the house started drawing return fire. When the room was silent from the men taking time to reload, I heard some musketballs striking the house. They must have been luck shots from afar, as no Yanks were close enough to see the Rebels in the windows. Later, though, a cannonball hit one of the front porch columns, and I heard it crack. George heard it, too, and said come with him into the hallway. I sat with George a bit, then went downstairs. I don't know what I was thinking, but after about ten minutes I went back up to sit with George again.

Everything I just wrote took place yesterday. Now it's late morning of a new day. A minute or two ago I ran down the hill, then came straight back. The good news is that Captain Nelson is unharmed. The bad news is that Brigadier General Cobb and the Georgia boy I wrote about are dead. Brigadier General Cobb was Captain Nelson's commander. There are other Rebel dead, too, but nowhere near the number of dead Yanks in the field beyond the wall. There are thousands of Yank bodies in plain view, and that is aside from any that were carried away. The sight of those Yanks is more than horrible, as last night some Rebels crept into the field and took all the coats and boots they could gather. Now the Yanks are not only dead, but half-naked, too. I know the cold made the Rebels do what they did; still it seems shameful to rob dead men.

Everyone is amazed the Yanks did not renew the attack today. They must have lost the spirit for fighting, having been stung so bad beyond the stone wall.

There was some shooting down the hill this afternoon, but it was not steady and amounted to nothing after yesterday.

Later

It's dusk now and I am reminded of the sun yesterday afternoon. It was red like I've never seen or heard of before. All the smoke rising from the guns must explain the strange color. Still, it was spooky to see a red sun in the sky on a day when so much blood was spilled on the ground. I'll always remember it as some sort of sad sign from heaven.

Corporal Welsh told me the general for the North Carolina troops was killed yesterday not long after Brigadier General Cobb died. That leaves both regiments without a leader now, which is terrible news. It could be worse though. At least the men held the wall, and the two generals did not die for nothing.

I am past tired and am going to sleep early. It is biting cold again tonight.

December 15

It is raining tonight and I have a bad case of the shivers. Even so, I ought not complain as I have a roof over my head while most of the soldiers do not. At least it is not so cold as before.

The Yanks sent a flag of truce this afternoon for burying the dead and tending the wounded. It was accepted by Robert E. Lee and the terrible task of digging graves has begun. The Yanks have more work than the Rebels by far. No one knows how many Union soldiers are dead, for they are still counting, but Captain Nelson estimated the Yanks lost upwards of six thousand men opposite the stone wall alone. That's an amazing high number. The Rebel dead behind the stone wall comes to eight hundred.

When you think no one wants to die and so many did, it's hard to understand the meaning of what happened here. The Confederates won the battle on Saturday, but what did they win? If you were close to one of the men who died, you would not feel as if you had won much. Maybe that's what war is. You lose when you lose and lose when you win.

I want to relate an interesting tale Captain Nelson told me. The only fighting yesterday was in the afternoon, when the Yanks took one more try for the stone wall. They started across the open field like before and the Rebels pinned them down in the field so they could not move for hours. The Yanks were lying there unable to get up and run, for the Rebel sharpshooters were at the ready. From time to time, some Yanks broke from cover and ventured into the field to assist their comrades, but most of them did not get far before Rebel shooting drove them back. Captain Nelson said it was brave of those Yanks who tried to help the men in the field, and most of the Rebel sharpshooters felt the same, for they aimed high and wide on purpose when they drove the Yanks back. It seems a strange sort of respect to show for an enemy, especially after all the killing that previously took place. Or maybe it is not so strange when you think that everyone on both sides is just a human. Captain Nelson said he had heard talk of a South Carolina boy from the Rebel side going into the field to carry water to some of the fallen Yanks, but he did not personally witness the event. I guess it goes to prove that some people keep their decency no matter how ugly the situation.

Anyhow, looking back to what happened at the wall on Saturday, I must say that the Yanks who charged across the field were made of some pretty stern stuff.

Despite the noise of the rain, I can hear a wounded Rebel screaming in the house. He keeps hollering, "Help me, Gawd. Help me." There are some doctors in there with a few of the wounded, and I guess they are pulling a slug out of that soldier. Or maybe they are cutting something off, which is what they do when there is no chance for proper healing.

I don't know how George can stand sleeping over there. I would rather shiver out here in the damp stable than sleep in a dry house with a hollering man.

December 16

Everybody is talking about how the Yanks retreated last night out of Fredericksburg. They were barricaded in the streets yesterday evening at dusk, showing no sign of preparing to attack, but showing no sign of retreating, either. Then this morning when the sun came up, they were gone across the river. No one here expected them to leave and many are regretting that such a large number of enemy got away without being pursued. The Rebels have now reclaimed the town.

Brompton looks bad. It is all shot up, with broken windows and the porch hanging free on one side. Mister Marye will not be happy when he returns and sees the shape his house is in. About noon today I was standing with George looking at the house when a meal wagon arrived in the yard and clanged the bell. I went with George to fetch a bowl from the kitchen, then stood in the line as if I were deserving. The cook sergeant gave me a sideways look, but did not say a counter word, and now I am full of pork and potatoes. I tried to return for a second helping to give to George, but the sergeant shooed me off. George claimed he never cared for pork anyway, but I know different. He only said that so I would not feel bad.

I'm running a fever that makes me hot, then cold. I've had such before and suspect I will be better soon.

December 18

I saw Robert E. Lee this morning when he rode over to commend Lieutenant General Longstreet and Major General MacLaws for their part in defending Fredericksburg. I could not get close, as there was a crowd of onlookers around General Lee. Even so, I sure enough saw him sitting straight-backed on Traveller. Maybe I am imagining things, but his face struck me as full of sadness for the slaughter that had taken place. His beard is whiter than I had thought. I am honored to see Robert E. Lee and will always remember today.

The reason I know General Lee commended Longstreet and MacLaws on fulfilling their duties is because Corporal Welsh was standing right there and heard what was said. The corporal also told me the dead had been more or less counted and the Federals lost almost thirteen thousand men in the fight. I did not have to ask who were the Federals, as I know it is another way of saying the Union Army. Thirteen thousand dead. That was a bad way for General Burnside to begin his command.

The dead on the Confederate side comes to five thousand two hundred and some. Adding that to the Yank dead means that more than eighteen thousand hearts have stopped beating forever. That's only the people. Lots of horses and mules died, too. Both sides will be busy digging graves for a week to come. The Rebels are burying most of their dead on a piece of flat land below the hill here, not far from the stone wall.

I wonder if the news has traveled to Bowling Green? Although I never said so, I suspect Momma knows I came to Fredericksburg and is worried for me. I will try somehow to get her a message.

Town is still off-limits to citizens, but I have decided to go look for Charlie Kent tomorrow. They can throw me in the brig if they want. I don't care.

DECEMBER 20

It's been two days since I wrote about going to look for Charlie Kent. I went yesterday like I said and, though I did not find Charlie, I met with Lieutenant Kershner and he said Charlie was alright. The lieutenant only happened to be in town delivering a report, as he and the others are stationed by the river now, north of town, so I was lucky to meet with him. He said he would give Charlie my regards and say I had survived the madness.

The town of Fredericksburg was ransacked by the Yanks and is a grim sight to behold. Many buildings are burned out and nearly all the rest have doors torn off and windows shattered. There is broken furniture in the streets and rubble piled up everywhere. Provost officers are guarding what property and valuables remain, although it is very little. After I spoke with Lieutenant Kershner, I was feeling so poorly I returned to Brompton.

December 25

I am sitting on the floor of the kitchen in Brompton and there is a fire burning in the cookstove. It is not a jolly Christmas for me. I have been so feverish these past days, I've hardly been able to speak, much less sit up to write in my journal. Even now I am so weak I had to rest after putting down the above three sentences. First I'm hot like lying in the sun during summer, then I'm cold like jumping in icy water. I don't know what ailment I have. George says I am down with swamp fever, but that does not seem likely to me. I did not argue with George, though, as I am mighty glad to have a friend looking after me while I'm ill.

LATER

I awoke a few minutes ago and drank a hot cup of broth. George said I'd been sleeping for nine hours. Corporal Welsh was here when I opened my eyes and the first thing he said was "Glad you're still with us, Rufus. There's been enough trouble around here for one month, without you getting sick and dying." I said I didn't aim to die, and he said, "You better not."

After Corporal Welsh left, George told me it was Corporal Welsh who carried me from the stable and made arrangements for me to sleep in the house. I guess word of my sickness has spread, as George also said that Captain Nelson had been by earlier. I hope he returns while I am awake.

I asked George if anything happened while I was sick and he said, "No, the Yanks are camping across the river the same as they were before they attacked Fredericksburg."

I hope Momma, Miss Brooks, Peg, Eveline, Charlie Kent, Captain Nelson, Corporal Welsh, George, and the little girl carrying her doll all had a Merry Christmas.

December 28

I am up and walking now, although not very strongly. There has been no fighting to report.

January 1, 1863

Here comes a new year and I don't know what I am going to do. The good news is, I've recovered from my sickness and am comfortably dressed, as all my clothes got washed and mended while I was down. When I tried to give George fifty cents for doing that, he said it was rude of me to offer. Later, if the stores open again, I aim to buy George some eggs and a bag of licorice. He told me before he has never tasted licorice.

I finally saw Captain Nelson yesterday when he came for a brief visit. His regiment has been moved into town and he wasn't sure when he'd get another chance to come calling. I said I'd find him if I could, then he said it was nice knowing me and we shook hands. I don't know why, but I had a feeling when he went that we'd seen the last of each other. If that is so, I won't forget him, as his memory will always be in my mind with the fighting at the stone wall — and I couldn't forget that if I tried.

I just had another funny feeling that this new year that is starting will be full of good-byes for me.

January 4

Tomorrow is Monday, and I'm planning to pick up the business I was doing in town before the Yanks arrived. They're still camped across the river, but don't seem inclined to fight again soon.

Two days ago, President Lincoln signed that proclamation Miss Howlett told us about in September. Corporal Welsh said it has caused a lot of grumbling up North. After news of the Union losses in Fredericksburg was reported in the papers, the pacifist movement began arguing for President Lincoln to negotiate boundaries and let the South go. Meanwhile, the abolitionists keep shouting for the South to be destroyed. I don't know how they expect President Lincoln to do such, as so far the Yanks have mostly just destroyed themselves.

Of course, to be completely honest, there has been plenty of destruction on the Rebel side as well. Win or lose, war puts an awful strain on everyone's posterity.

JANUARY 5

There was no business to be done in town. The citizens have not been allowed to return and no stores are open for making purchases. The streets are full of soldiers resting and licking their wounds, and some of them are working to clean up the mess. They all looked haggard to me, no matter what they were doing. The strange thing was, I did not see a single familiar face. I guess the Mississippi bunch has moved elsewhere.

JANUARY 12

I have not put down a word for eight days because there has been nothing to write. All everyone around here is doing is trying to stay warm and waiting to see what the Yanks will do. It's not an easy time and some of the men have taken to cursing a lot. There are only two or three in ten that use foul language, but that's all it takes to throw a poor impression on the whole army. It seems strange to me that Rebel soldiers can praise Robert E. Lee in one breath, then curse as they do in the next. I'm not saying the men ought to pretend they're in church, but maybe more should follow the mannerly example of General Robert E. Lee.

According to Corporal Welsh, the Union Army has been hit with a slew of desertions. He said some Yanks are leaving in disagreement with the Emancipation Proclamation, and some are leaving because of Burnside's deadly leadership here in Fredericksburg, but most Yanks were going to get away from the miserable living conditions that have been making people sick. It can be hard living in a tent during winter. I know, as I took ill when I had a dry room to sleep in. My feeling is that most of the quitters just want a hot meal. It doesn't take long to go sour on hardtack and buggy gruel.

I have made no decision, but lately I've begun to think of leaving here soon. With no business to do in town, and Charlie Kent and Captain Nelson who knows where, I find myself just loitering around Brompton in the cold. I can't say I miss Bowling Green or anything like that, but sometimes I figure if I'm doing nothing, I might as well be learning something in school.

JANUARY 14

Mister Marye was here this morning to speak with some officers and survey the damage to his house. He came on horseback and did not stay long. There was part of me that wanted to ask after Peg and Eveline, but instead I thought it wise to hide until after Mister Marye had departed. His being here just reminds me I don't belong at Brompton in the first place. Except for George and Corporal Welsh, there is nothing holding me here but a dry room to stay in.

JANUARY 17

I went today and sat on the town side of the railroad bridge. The Rebels took it down to stop the Yanks from gaining control of the southbound tracks. If the Yanks did that they could ride straight from Washington to Richmond, instead of trying to fight their way through Virginia.

The wind was up and I was holding my hat when I looked across the river and saw a man where the bridge drops off on the other side. It took me a while to figure out what he was doing, but then I saw he had a camera and was taking a picture of me. At first that made me feel strange, as I've never been in a photograph before, but then I thought maybe the man works for a Northern newspaper and my picture would be on the front page. They wouldn't know who I was and might write something like, "Daring Rebel Scout Disguised as Normal Civilian Keeps Eye on Union Troops." It is true, I was watching the Yanks, and while doing so I got the impression they were packing up and preparing to move.

This evening I told Corporal Welsh what I observed about the Yanks and he said he'd report the matter to Colonel Walton. He is one of the officers living in Brompton. Colonel Walton reports to Major General MacLaws, who answers to Lieutenant General Longstreet. Anyway, the corporal told me thank you for the information.

LATER

For some reason, the idea of soaking in a hot tub of water has gotten on my mind and I can't get it off. It leads me to think more about maybe going home to visit Momma. The only good thing about her marrying Mister Jenkins is his house, which has a separate room for bathing in a copper tub. There's a fireplace in the room, too. I used to get the fire roaring hot during winter, then sit in the tub and pretend I was bathing somewhere in the summertime. I do miss that luxury.

If I did go home, Momma would be heartened to see me. Probably the worst that could happen would be Mister Jenkins saying I left home once and cannot come back again. All I'd have lost then would be a twenty-mile walk, and at least I would've been able to tell Momma I was alright. She deserves to know that much.

JANUARY 18

Today is Sunday and I told George I was fixing to leave Brompton. He asked when I was going. I was preparing to say right now, but then he looked so concerned waiting for my answer, I said I didn't know when, but sometime soon. His forehead got all wrinkled, then he allowed that going home was not a dumb thing to do. I like George's gentle manner. I have not forgotten my intention of buying him a bag of licorice and some eggs.

JANUARY 19

It snowed last night while everyone was sleeping and was still snowing when I went out this morning. That was before the hilltop got trampled into a mess and everything was still smoothed over in white. After all the dying that took place around here recently, the white color gave me a hopeful feeling. The snow picked up more spirits than mine, too.

There was a huge snowball fight today at Brompton. It commenced before noon and went on for a good two hours. No one is willing to agree on the matter, but I think the fight was started by the Washington Artillery. It was them against the younger officers from the house, plus some infantry men and me. I teamed with Corporal Welsh. We had a high time until he took two snowballs in the face and quit.

It's just a crazy thought, but wouldn't it be nice if the Yanks and Rebels could settle their differences with a huge snowball fight? That would save a lot of wear and tear, and misery.

JANUARY 20

Early this morning Corporal Welsh came to my room to report that my observations about the Yanks had proven correct, as the whole Union Army had packed up in the night and was presently beginning to move. I joshed was I going to get paid for my spy work. He said no, but did I want to go with him to watch the Federals depart? We walked to a spot above town where we could see across to Falmouth, which is where the main action was taking place. A crowd of Rebels was already there when we arrived. The Yanks had bands playing as the infantry lined up in their units and there were cavalrymen flying their regimental colors. It was a genuine spectacle. Plenty of Rebels were hollering at the Yanks, saying how glad they were to see them go. Then two soldiers came with a sign they had made and waved it at the Yanks. The sign said, "This way to Richmond." It caused an outbreak of merriment on our side of the river. Some men laughed so hard they had to hold their knees to keep from falling.

We watched the Yanks for nearly three hours. They have so many cannons and wagons to move, and regiments and divisions to follow one after another, some soldiers were still standing where they'd started when Corporal Welsh and I grew tired of watching and returned to Brompton.

It's evening now. It was warm all day. A little while ago it started to rain.

January 21

Rain was pouring down this morning and is still falling at five o'clock in the evening as I write this. I went today to see how the Yanks had fared with their departure from Falmouth. Most of them had moved on when I got to where Corporal Welsh and I were standing yesterday, but the supply wagons and the back end of the army was still in sight. They were struggling in the mess left by all the traffic that went ahead. It was a big mess, too, as the ground had thawed, and it had been raining steady for more than fifteen hours, and there was nothing underfoot but soupy mud to travel over. I dare say, on a dry day I could hop backward on one leg faster than the Yanks were moving out of Falmouth.

After watching the back end of the Union Army for an hour or so, I hiked along the riverbank toward a place called U.S. Ford, where the Rebels were protecting against a crossing. Before I got half that far I could see the main body of the Yanks bogged down in confusion behind a cannon and two mules stuck in a mud pit. The troops behind could not pass, and so with the troops behind them, and the whole time the rain never let up. The Yanks were obviously frustrated with the situation and looked a far cry less proud than they did yesterday when they marched off with their bands playing. Some of the Yank soldiers were sitting in the mud, appearing as if they'd drop over any minute. I saw two Yanks break away from their division and straggle into the woods across from where I stood. They noticed me on the riverbank watching them, but paid me no mind. I reckon all they cared about was finding a dry place to hide.

It continues to rain tonight. I spoke with Corporal Welsh this evening and told him where I'd gone and what I'd seen today. He said he'd spent the day with Colonel Walton obtaining supplies at Spotsylvania Courthouse.

I pulled the slips of paper out of my coat and my shoe. The one from my shoe was damaged so I burned it over a candle. I was going to do the same with the other, but then I reckoned it takes nothing to carry my name with me, and I put it back in my coat.

★★★

JANUARY 23

The Yanks turned around yesterday and returned to their old camps across the river from Fredericksburg. That's twice in a row they've been beat. First by General Robert E. Lee and the Confederate Army. Second by the Virginia mud.

LATER

I started thinking again about having a hot bath and seeing Momma, and a short while ago made my decision to leave tomorrow. As soon as my mind was made, I went to tell George what I planned. I feared he'd take my leaving hard, but he appeared relieved and agreed it was wise for me to go. I told him I'd probably return in the spring to visit and he said, "You're welcome anytime, Rufus, but don't rush back if the war is still on. We were lucky together during this last mess, but luck ought never be pressed. Do you understand what I say?" I answered, "Yes sir, and I hope we are lucky apart, too." George chuckled at that. Then we shook hands and I came to write this down. Only thing left for me to do now is find Corporal Welsh in the morning and say good-bye to him.

JANUARY 25

I said good-bye to Corporal Welsh before leaving Brompton on Saturday morning. I walked all day and reached Bowling Green before dark. The roads were muddy and it was a hard walk, which I figure at twenty-two miles. Along the way I was thinking some may consider my return home to be a defeat, but then I never made any claims about my departure and, the fact is, I've had an adventure I will not soon forget.

Momma and Mister Jenkins were sitting down to dinner when I appeared at the door. Both were much surprised to see me. Momma cried and held on to me like I was risen from the dead. She wouldn't let go until I told her I needed to sit, as I'd been walking all day. She kept asking questions about where I'd been and how I'd survived. The whole while Mister Jenkins just sat there quietly. After a sharp look from Momma, he said, "I reckon you're hungry, boy," and went to fix me a plate of chicken, applesauce, green beans, and potatoes. I remembered then that we always ate big on Saturday nights and counted myself lucky.

After I ate and Momma quit fussing over me, she went to build up a fire and boil water so I could have a bath. At that time Mister Jenkins confessed to have been worrying so much the last few years about his timbering business that he'd lost sight of giving some people their proper respect. It was his way of apologizing for the way he'd behaved toward me, and I told him I believed bygones were bygones. So for now we have a truce between us. I hope it holds, but I'll be surprised if it does, as the man still has a mean look in his eye toward me.

LATER

It's strange the turns that life can take. Yesterday I was hungry and cold and worried about my welcome home, and today I'm warm, clean from a bath, and lazy from eating too much. I never felt better waking up in a bed than I did this morning. The only drawback to my happiness is knowing the hardship my friends in Fredericksburg are facing.

Maybe having rickets gave me the luck to not wear a uniform, as otherwise I'd be shivering now in a tent, or dead.

JANUARY 26

If you stretch out in a mile circle, Bowling Green only has three hundred citizens, so it was easy for everyone to know of my return. After school let out this afternoon Gertrude and Anne Furr came rushing to the house to see me. They didn't know what to say after hello and welcome home, and they just stood looking at me for a long time. I'd nearly forgotten how much I like Gertrude. She turned twelve while I was away. She always looked up to me in school because I used to help her on occasion with her reading. Anne is Gertrude's little sister and follows her everywhere. They were so shy looking at me, the attention made me blush. They left when Miss Howlett presented herself at the door. I feared

84

she might be angry at me for having quit on her, but the opposite was true. She stated that she hoped to see me back in school when I was rested and felt up to coming. Miss Howlett's action was one to respect and I told her I'd come soon.

That was all yesterday. Tonight Momma and Mister Jenkins and I sat around the fire after dinner. They were so curious about me seeing Robert E. Lee and the fighting in Fredericksburg, my tongue got tired from answering questions. Momma suggested I write things down before I get old and forget them. I told her I was keeping this journal.

JANUARY 27

I returned to school today and Miss Howlett asked if I would stand before the class and speak of my experiences. I said yes, and then she said let's wait until afternoon because she wanted to invite a few folks she knew would be curious. So at two o'clock when I spoke to the class, there were six adults standing in the back of the room listening. All had questions and were desperate for firsthand news.

When I was done, my old friend, Thornton Scott, came to shake my hand and said I'd done something brave. While he was doing so I saw Gertrude watching me as if I were a big hero. I will not let such popularity go to my head.

FEBRUARY 1

Today is Sunday and Thornton Scott stopped by the house to give me Friday's edition of the *Richmond Enquirer*, which he bought on Saturday when the stagecoach passed through. He said I should have it, as there was an interesting piece on President Lincoln having removed General Burnside from command of the Union Army on January 25.

The newspaper allowed that General Burnside did give a fight, which was more than could be said for General McClellan before him, but he hesitated too long and afterward made too many mistakes to keep the confidence of the Union troops. The newspaper also said Burnside had been falling apart personally, but I don't know how anyone from Richmond could know that. Anyway, there was a long piece on what the paper called "The Mud March" back and forth from Falmouth, which took place between January 20 and January 22. The story was pretty much true, but it was apparent to me the reporter had not been present at the scene. The man would've benefited from speaking with me before writing the piece, as I could've supplied him with many details.

The command that General Burnside lost was given to a general named Joe Hooker, whom the Yanks call "Fighting Joe." He takes over an unhappy army. The newspaper estimated that eighty thousand Yank soldiers have recently abandoned their posts. I doubt if Fighting Joe will have better luck against General Robert E. Lee than the other generals.

Another piece in the newspaper spoke about the falling worth of the Confederate dollar. It has dropped to twenty cents against the hundred it was worth before the War started. That seems odd to me, as the Rebels are winning, but that's what has happened. I'm glad I took copper and silver in Fredericksburg, so my money has not lost so much value.

February 11

I've been sharing newspapers with Thornton Scott and keeping a keen eye for news from Fredericksburg. There has been little. General Hooker and the Union Army still sit across the river at Falmouth. There have been some skirmishes north of town, but no big fights.

February 14

Both the *Richmond Enquirer* and the *Richmond Examiner* have been reporting on the great success of the Confederate Cavalry, which has been on regular raids behind the Union lines. The newspapers tell of how the Confederates know every nook and cranny in the woods, and how women and children have been warning the Rebels when the Yanks are lying in wait. The stories remind me of the fat man I saw in the Rising Sun Tavern who was bragging on Jeb Stuart. I wish I'd seen Jeb Stuart during my time in Fredericksburg, but I did not. I'll just have to live with having seen Robert E. Lee, Lafayette MacLaws, and James Longstreet. That's more than anyone else from Bowling Green can claim.

FEBRUARY 17

Miss Howlett has proven to be an effective teacher and has been lending me books to read over and above regular homework. She claims that I demonstrate above-average skills with my letters and that I would be wise to concentrate in that area for my future. I think she advises me so on account of my rickets having left me unfit for a life of labor. Still, I take her interest as a compliment and have enjoyed one book she lent me in particular. It's called *Gulliver's Travels* and was written by a humorous fellow named Jonathan Swift.

FEBRUARY 21

There was a report in the *Richmond Examiner* of the Confederate Army withdrawing several divisions from positions overlooking Fredericksburg last

Wednesday and Thursday. There were no facts on which troops were withdrawn or where they went, but Brompton overlooks the town and I wonder if it was General Longstreet's division that departed. Major General MacLaws is under him, and Corporal Welsh is way down under MacLaws, so maybe Corporal Welsh has gone. The news reminds me of him and George.

February 22

I told Momma this afternoon that I was thinking of paying a visit to some folks that were good to me in Fredericksburg. She looked at me as if I'd poked her with a hot iron and said please do not consider such a thing. I replied that I only meant to go for two or three days at most to give my respects and asked her what harm that would do. She said it would do plenty harm to her heart, which had just gotten used to having me home again. Then she said if I wanted to give my respects, why didn't I write a letter like most people who are separated do. I walked away hot when Momma said that, but then I cooled down and went back to tell her I wouldn't go anywhere until the War was over. I feel mixed about giving her my word.

Mister Jenkins and I have been steering clear of each other and so far have had no problems. That doesn't mean I trust him enough to let down my guard. It just means nothing bad has happened yet. Anyhow, I reckon I'll just settle for the time being and keep with my studies.

MARCH 8

I took Momma's suggestion and wrote to Corporal Welsh, telling him that I was safe at home and how much everyone wanted to hear of what I'd seen in Fredericksburg. I wrote that I remembered him and George fondly and would try to locate each of them after the War. I realized while writing that I never did catch Corporal Welsh's first name, so I addressed the envelope like this: To Corporal Welsh, Brompton, MacLaws' division of Confederate Army, Fredericksburg, Virginia. After the news of troops being moved from positions overlooking town, I have no way of knowing if the letter will be received. Even so, I hope for a reply with each southbound stagecoach that passes through Bowling Green. They used to run regular up and down the turnpike, but now only come once or twice a week, and some weeks not at all.

Thornton Scott watches the mails and promises to deliver any letters that arrive for me.

April 12

It's been well over a month since I wrote anything here. That's mostly because nothing ever happens in Bowling Green and also because there has been no major action in the War. That appears fixing to change, though, as Thornton Scott told me this evening there was a rumor the Yanks were moving a number of troops from Falmouth. He heard so from a coach driver traveling south from Spotsylvania Courthouse. The man had not been in Fredericksburg and knew nothing of the situation there, but said he reckoned the Yanks were preparing to sweep around the Confederates and advance on Richmond.

That is nothing new. People have been speculating the Yanks would rush to Richmond since the Union Army marched out of Washington more than a year ago.

April 14

It was Momma's birthday today and we celebrated with a pot roast dinner, which is her favorite meal. The skies were blue all day and it is warm this evening like summertime.

April 15

The Richmond newspapers tell of General Longstreet's division beginning a siege of Suffolk, Virginia. If that is so, then he is no longer in Fredericksburg, which means that Corporal Welsh likely missed my letter. That is a disappointment, as one of the main reasons for that letter was George hearing what I wrote. I hope he doesn't think I've forgotten him. I suspect not, as George is a faithful sort.

April 19

Miss Howlett lent me a book called *Poor Richard's Almanack* that I began reading two days ago. It was written by Benjamin Franklin and contains a lot of plain speaking about how to consider life and handle different circumstances. There are some funny parts, too, which impresses me, as Mister Franklin completed *Poor Richard's Almanack* more than one hundred years ago. Mister Franklin also helped write the Declaration of Independence.

This journal that Miss Brooks gave me is running out of empty pages and I must be careful how I use the remaining ones.

May 4

Thornton Scott stopped by the house an hour ago with a load of news, some of it awful. Stonewall Jackson was shot by one of his own men out near Chancellorsville, which is no more than eight miles west of Fredericksburg. It was an accident at night. The general was returning to camp and a Rebel picket mistook him for a Yank and shot him off his horse. The general is said to be a strong man, which gives hope he may recover. His real name is Thomas Jackson and he comes from Lexington, Virginia. Robert E. Lee gave him the nickname of Stonewall at the Battle of Bull Run.

There is some better news. The day and evening of May 2, the same night Stonewall Jackson was shot, he was out with a division that circled secretly behind Fighting Joe Hooker's army. This came after two days of heavy fighting. While Robert E. Lee held General Hooker's forward attention with hardly a quarter of the soldiers that Hooker had, Stonewall Jackson attacked the Union troops from behind and threw them into great confusion. The grass in the fields where the Yanks were sitting was dry and caught fire in many places when Stonewall Jackson's division attacked.

No one yet knows the number of dead at Chancellorsville, but it was many, and most were Yanks.

The other bad news after Stonewall Jackson being shot is that while the two sides were fighting at Chancellorsville, a Yank commander named Sedgwich attacked the town of Fredericksburg with more than twenty thousand soldiers. Thornton and I tried to figure out which Rebels had been in town to defend Fredericksburg, but were unable to guess. With Longstreet laying siege in Suffolk and Robert E. Lee and Stonewall Jackson engaged at Chancellorsville, it could not have been a large force. I suggested maybe Major General MacLaws was heading the defense.

The news leaves me with a lot to ponder. I hope George's luck continues to hold.

MAY 5

The stagecoach did not appear in Bowling Green this evening when hoped for. That is no surprise, but it's a disappointment not to hear news about Fredericksburg or word on how Stonewall Jackson is faring.

MAY 7

Bad news. Thornton Scott got ahold of the *Richmond Examiner* when he was in Ashland yesterday and it reports that Brompton was taken by the Yanks. In the paper they call it Marye's Heights, but that is the hill that Brompton sits upon and so must be the same. The newspaper told of all-day fighting before the Heights was taken. It said the Rebels defending Marye's Heights were under Jubal Early. I've never heard of him before, but the *Examiner* reported that Early and his men put up fierce resistance against a much larger Union force. Some of Robert E. Lee's troops appeared the next day and the Yanks retreated over to Falmouth where General Hooker had run after losing at Chancellorsville.

I don't know what to imagine for George. I hope he gave up watching the house before the Yanks took over. Maybe he hid in the cupboard he knew of below the stairs.

The newspaper also carried the story about Stonewall Jackson being accidentally shot by one of his own men. It added some facts I had not known, such as the picket who shot Stonewall Jackson being from North Carolina and one of the general's arms being amputated the night of the accident. I must say, the notion of having an arm sawed off is horrible to behold. Still, I reckon it beats dying.

I've never been what anyone would call a religious person, but tonight I aim to get on my knees and pray for George and Stonewall Jackson, and for Charlie Kent and Captain Nelson, and for Peg and Eveline, and for Corporal Welsh and everybody else I know.

MAY 8

Thornton Scott's cousin William rode through Bowling Green this morning on his way to Hanover. He was coming from Spotsylvania Courthouse, which is hardly a stone's throw from Chancellorsville. William told Thornton the two days of fighting at Chancellorsville were the bloodiest since Antietam Creek and that Robert E. Lee was receiving credit for outsmarting Fighting Joe Hooker. I guess so, as Robert E. Lee won the field with forty-five thousand Rebels going against ninety thousand Yanks.

When I heard that William said Chancellorsville was the bloodiest after Antietam Creek, I wondered how it could've been worse than the slaughter occurring in Fredericksburg this past December. Then Thornton told me the early count was more than eighteen thousand Yank dead and eleven thousand Rebel dead.

I find it impossible to see that number of soldiers in my mind, much less think of them all dead. It nearly breaks my heart, as I know each man had a name and probably some friends and a mother living somewhere. I don't believe the killing can continue at this rate without one side soon wishing to quit.

MAY 9

Thornton Scott was here this evening to say that Stonewall Jackson is being cared for over near Guinea. That is in Caroline County, not more than ten miles from where I sit now. Thornton said an infection had gotten into General Jackson and the man was ailing so, his wife had traveled to his side.

Thornton believes he knows the house where Stonewall Jackson lies. We aim to seek it out tomorrow morning, which is Sunday. Not owning a horse of my own, I'll have to ride double with Thornton.

I've always been a little frightened of horses, and I am more so now after running into that dead one when I was retreating from the stone wall. Still, I won't allow fear to hold me back from paying respects to Stonewall Jackson. I just hope he doesn't die. That would be a terrible loss.

May 11

I stayed home from school today. I'm sick with sadness because Stonewall Jackson died yesterday afternoon. I know because I was standing in the yard outside the little house where the great man spent his last hour. I heard his wife wail when he went and the sound jabbed in my chest. There were more than a dozen men and soldiers in the yard at the time, and to the last of us we all got tears in our eyes. I almost thought I could keep from sobbing out loud, but then a captain who had been in the house came out and told us Stonewall Jackson's last words. The last thing the general said on earth was, "No, no. Let us pass over the river and rest under the shade of the trees." When I heard that I broke down grieving without control.

I've now covered the next to final page in my journal. It's hard to believe I wrote so much, but then I think of all that passed since September and know there was more I might've put down. If I could change the truth, I wouldn't finish with Stonewall Jackson dying. I'd have him recover and return to Robert E. Lee's aid.

June 3

I'd forgotten this final page until today when I was bored and decided to read some of my journal. Two weeks ago I had a short letter from Corporal Welsh saying he received my letter in early April and only now found time to reply. He'd recently returned to Fredericksburg with General Longstreet. Corporal Welsh had not gotten free to visit George on my behalf, but said he'd try soon if he could get away from his duties. Then he apologized for writing such a brief letter and signed his whole name.

That was good, for now I know him to be Woodford Covington Welsh. It makes me sort of proud to know a friend named Woodford who hails from Staunton, Virginia.

Rufus Rowe ended this journal on Wednesday, June 3, in the year eighteen sixty-three.

EPILOGUE

★ ★ ★

As he had promised his mother, Rufus Rowe remained in Bowling Green until the end of the War. In May 1865, he traveled on foot to Fredericksburg and was pleased to find his friend George still in residence at Brompton, atop the hill known as Marye's Heights. Although now a free citizen, George had elected to remain in the employ of the Marye family and help the family with the difficult task of restoring their home. The house was in even worse shape than Rufus remembered, as it had been occupied after his departure by Union troops and used as a field hospital.

Although Rufus and George were both glad to see each other, their reunion was short-lived and somewhat of a disappointment for Rufus. He presented George with a bag of licorice and the two sat for about forty minutes talking, during which time Rufus learned that Eveline remained at Forrest Hill with relatives and Peg had moved to Baltimore, where she'd taken a new position with another family. Then George was called back to work and the visit was over.

From Brompton, Rufus wandered into the town of Fredericksburg, where he considered seeking employment. However, after walking the streets for several hours and seeing no one he knew by name, Rufus left the town and walked back to Bowling Green that very night.

In early June 1865, Rufus received a letter from Woodford Welsh announcing his engagement to marry Liza Dunn Chapman in Staunton, Virginia, on Sunday, July 2. Woodford expressed his sincere desire that Rufus attend the wedding and invited Rufus to stay at the Welsh family farm for as long as he wished. Rufus promptly sat down and wrote to Woodford that he would be there if he could.

Via stagecoach and rail, Rufus traveled from Bowling Green, Virginia, to Staunton, Virginia, and attended the wedding of Liza Chapman and Woodford Welsh. While there, Rufus fell into conversation with an employee of the Southern Pacific Railroad and learned that the company was looking for telegraph operators in their New Orleans offices. Although not formally instructed in Morse code, Rufus had read a book on the new language and decided he would seek one of the open positions. Using the last of his personal savings, he traveled to Louisiana and talked his way into a job with the Southern Pacific Railroad.

Rufus lived and worked as a telegraph operator in New Orleans for three years and four months. He enjoyed his independence and was able to save a fair amount of money during his employment, yet was forever homesick for the Old Dominion.

In February 1869, Rufus resigned from his position with the Southern Pacific Railroad and returned to Bowling Green. There he quickly grew bored and, less than a month after returning home, he moved to Richmond, Virginia. It was here that Rufus' true destiny awaited. Lucky Rufus: Within a week of his arrival in the state capital he was hired as a cub reporter for the *Richmond Enquirer.*

One day, approximately five weeks after Rufus began living and working in Richmond, he was walking on Church Hill when he heard someone call his name. He turned and — to his delight — saw his much adored, former teacher, Miss Brooks, now known as Mrs. Ashton Gray. In the course of renewing their old friendship, Rufus reminded Mrs. Gray of the leather-bound book she'd given him before her departure from Bowling Green and asked if she would like to read what he'd written. She said yes, of course, and then could not put it down once she started to read.

LIFE IN AMERICA
IN 1862

HISTORICAL NOTE

★ ★ ★

When thinking about the Civil War it is important to remember that it was fought less than ninety years after the signing of the Declaration of Independence, a document proclaiming the formation of a free and indivisible nation. In the end, that nation — the United States — remained indivisible, but not before being tested by four years of bloodshed and economic devastation.

It was a ghastly war, principally fought as most wars are by young men, and one in which the combatants often stood close enough to look each other in the eye. It is estimated that more than six hundred thousand people lost their lives during the Civil War. More died of sickness than were killed in battle. For example, the Confederacy losses on the battlefield were approximately ninety-four thousand, and yet one hundred sixty-four thousand Confederate soldiers died from disease and improperly tended wounds.

The official Union designation for what we now think of as the Civil War was the "War of the Rebellion." The Confederate South called it the "War between the States," or the "War of Northern Aggression." It pitted the Blue against the Gray, the Yanks against the Rebels, Americans against Americans.

The period of the Civil War was a remarkably literate time in our nation. Never before had the ability to read and write been so widespread or — more importantly — so passionately pursued by such a large portion of the population. To the pleasure of both amateur historians and scholars interested in the Civil War, the writing of letters and keeping of journals was a popular activity with soldiers on both sides of the conflict. There was also a great abundance of daily newspapers printed during the War, many of which were easily available and read avidly by the troops in the fields.

During the latter months of 1862 and into the spring of 1863, it was reasonable for Rufus Rowe to believe the Confederate Army would prevail over the Union forces. The battle for Fredericksburg that Rufus witnessed was a tragic defeat for the Union. Perhaps if the bridge pontoons had arrived on time, the Union would have quickly taken control of Fredericksburg and used it as a forward base from which to march on the Confederate capital of Richmond. Perhaps: That is such a big word in matters of war.

At any rate, the bridges did not arrive in time and the Rebels successfully defended the town, leaving Rufus' optimism intact. Months later, at Chancellorsville, Robert E. Lee led the Confederates in a resounding victory over a Union force twice the size of his army. Although it was a battle in which Lee lost his good friend and most reliable commander, General Stonewall Jackson, the Union defeat at Chancellorsville boded well at the time for the Confederates.

The tide would turn the following summer when the Union won major victories in both Gettysburg and Vicksburg. From then on, the North held the upper hand in the War. However, by this time Rufus Rowe had completed his journal, so we do not know from him the despair of watching the South decline.

The town of Fredericksburg, Virginia, changed hands seven times between the firing of the first shot in the Civil War, on April 12, 1862, and Lee's surrender to Grant on April 9, 1865.

The house known as Brompton was still standing when the hostilities ended, and it was later restored by the Marye family. The house is currently owned by Mary Washington College. Below the hill is a Civil War visitor center maintained by the Federal Park Service.

A view of Fredericksburg, Virginia, in 1862.

Westover is one of the most famous plantation estates in Virginia. Originally established in 1619 by Lord Delaware, the estate was purchased by John Seldon in 1829. However, during the Civil War, Seldon fled, fearing the approach of Union soldiers. Union troops recognized the strategic benefits of the plantation, established a campground, and constructed an observation tower on the mansion roof. When the war ended, Westover was in ruins.

When General Ambrose E. Burnside took over command of the Union Army, he proposed a quick advance to Fredericksburg, Virginia. This maneuver would position the Union Army on the direct road to Richmond, the Confederate capital, and also provide a secure supply line to Washington.

The Union Army's swift attack on Fredericksburg left the Confederate Army at a disadvantage, as General Robert E. Lee, who had not anticipated the Union's advance on Fredericksburg, had divided his troops after the Maryland Campaign and was no longer in a position to defend the city.

Confederate soldiers found ready-made trenches behind the stone wall along
Telegraph Road.

Union forces were also entrenched along the bank of the Rappahannock River during the battle at Fredericksburg.

This composite portrays Confederate commanders Jefferson Davis, James Longstreet, J.E.B. Stewart, Stonewall Jackson, Robert E. Lee, Joseph Johnston, P.G.T. Beauregard, and others.

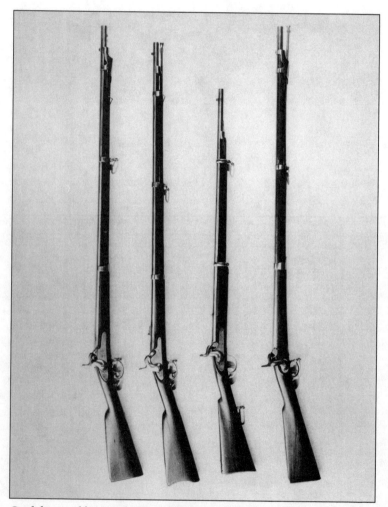

Confederate soldiers used several different types of rifles, including the Palmetteo Musket, the Confederate Richmond Rifle Musket, the Confederate Cook Infantry rifle, and the Morse Musket.

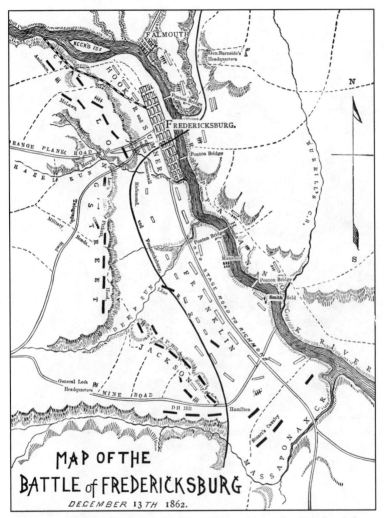

MAP OF THE
BATTLE of FREDERICKSBURG
DECEMBER 13TH 1862.

This map shows the positioning of troops during the Battle of Fredericksburg, Virginia, in 1862.

Fredericksburg was in ruins after the battle there. Buildings were destroyed and bore the pockmarks of cannon and musket fire.

Union soldiers who were wounded at the Battle of Fredericksburg found medical care and shelter in a nearby farmhouse.

About the Author

★ ★ ★

"I grew up in a small town located about halfway between Fredericksburg and Richmond, Virginia," writes Sid Hite. "I would have needed to pass my entire childhood with wax in my ears to avoid hearing stories about the Civil War. Thus, when I was asked to write a book for the My Name Is America series, I did not have to look far for my subject. Rufus's story takes place in some of the very same places that I spent my youth in and around Bowling Green, Virginia."

Sid Hite is the author of seven critically acclaimed novels, including *Stick and Whittle*, which was named a New York Public Library Book for the Teen Age and a Smithsonian Notable Book for Children, and *A Hole in the World*, which is his latest book for Scholastic. *The Journal of Rufus Rowe* is his first book for the My Name Is America line.

FOR JANET AND GLENN GIBSON

Acknowledgments

★ ★ ★

Grateful acknowledgment is made for permission to reprint the following:

Cover Portrait: Maximilian Cabanas, Bettman/CORBIS.

Cover Background: Jackson's Confederate Army, North Wind Pictures, Alfred, Maine.

Page 115: View of Fredericksburg, Culver Pictures, New York.
Page 116: Westover Plantation, The Corcoran Gallery of Art/CORBIS, New York.
Page 117: Advance on Fredericksburg, Culver Pictures, New York.
Page 118: Union Army's attack on Fredericksburg, Library of Congress via Scholastic Online Digital Archives.
Page 119: Confederate soldiers behind the stone wall, North Wind Pictures, Alfred, Maine.

Page 120: Entrenched Union soldiers, Medford Historical
Society Collection/CORBIS, New York.

Page 121: Confederate commanders, CORBIS.

Page 122: Confederate rifles, Bettman/CORBIS.

Page 123: Map of the Battle of Fredericksburg, North
Wind Pictures, Alfred, Maine.

Page 124: Fredericksburg in ruins, North Wind Pictures,
Alfred, Maine.

Page 125: Wounded Union soldiers, Culver Pictures,
New York.

OTHER BOOKS IN THE MY NAME IS AMERICA SERIES

The Journal of William Thomas Emerson
A Revolutionary War Patriot
by Barry Denenberg

The Journal of James Edmond Pease
A Civil War Union Soldier
by Jim Murphy

The Journal of Joshua Loper
A Black Cowboy
by Walter Dean Myers

The Journal of Scott Pendleton Collins
A World War II Soldier
by Walter Dean Myers

The Journal of Sean Sullivan
A Transcontinental Railroad Worker
by William Durbin

Copyright © 2003 by Sid Hite

✫✫✫

Library of Congress Cataloging-in-Publication Data

Hite, Sid.
The journal of Rufus Rowe : witness to the Battle of Fredericksburg /
by Sid Hite.
p.   cm.—(My Name Is America)
Summary: In 1862, sixteen-year-old Rufus Rowe runs away from
home and settles in Fredericksburg, Virginia, where he documents in
his journal the battle he watches unfold there.

ISBN 0-439-35364-5

[1. Fredericksburg, Battle of, Fredericksburg, Va., 1862—Juvenile Fiction.
2. Fredericksburg, Battle of, Fredericksburg, Va., 1862—Fiction.
3. Diaries—Fiction. 4. United States—History—Civil War,
1861–1865—Fiction.] I. Title. II. Series.
PZ7.H62964 Jo 2003
[Fic] 21   2002044577
                           CIP   AC

10 9 8 7 6 5 4 3 2   03 04 05 06 07

The display type was set in Old Claude Small Caps.
The text type was set in Berling Roman.
Book design by Elizabeth B. Parisi.
Photo research by Amla Sanghvi.

Printed in the U.S.A   23
First printing, October 2003

✫✫✫